Theobold the Iron-Hearted

Originally Published in 1871
By
E. Thompson Baird

Grace & Truth Books
Sand Springs, Oklahoma

ISBN # 1-58339-058-8
First printings, 1871
Printed by Triangle Press, 1993
Current printing, Grace & Truth Books, 2003

Cover design by Ben Gundersen

Grace & Truth Books
3406 Summit Boulevard
Sand Springs, Oklahoma   74063
Phone: 918 245 1500

www.graceandtruthbooks.com
email: gtbooksorders@cs.com

Table of Contents

Page

Forward

Chapter 1 - The Wounded Knight . . 1

Chapter 2 - An Enemy Treated Kindly. . 7

Chapter 3 - Love Your Enemies . . 13

Chapter 4 - The Lion Returns . . . 23

Chapter 5 - Erhard's Account of the Conflict 31

Chapter 6 - A Secret Revealed . . . 39

Chapter 7 - A Joyous Surprise . . . 43

Chapter 8 - Enemies United . . . 49

*They could see from the top of the steep hill, some
troops were still fighting.*

Chapter 1

The Wounded Knight

Two hostile armies met in 1423 in the long and gruesome war which followed the martyrdom of John Huss and Jerome of Prague. They met in the most beautiful valley of Bohemia. John Huss and Jerome of Prague had both been burned alive at Constance. This order came from the council held in that city. The first execution would be on the 6th of July, in 1415. The second would be on the 30th of May, in 1416.

The battle began towards the close of day and continued until after sunset.

It was then that old Erik, accompanied by Franz, his grandson, climbed to the top of a steep hill. They could see from the edge, in the depth of the valley behind a wood, some troops were still fighting.

The old man and the child (Franz was scarcely nine years of age) were sad and silent. They both looked towards the plain. "Oh, how good is the Lord, if He has preserved my father!" said Franz with a deep sigh.

"The Lord can preserve him," Erik said solemnly. "Erhard belongs to Him. Yes, my son, your father is one of God's dear children."

"Grandpa," resumed Franz, looking at the old man, "do not Christians also die in battle? God does not preserve them all."

"If my son has laid down his life for the Lord," continued Erik, "he is not dead. His soul has gone from this world to be with his Saviour."

"To be with mama!" said the child. "In heaven with the angels, isn't that right, dear Grandpa?"

"To be with your mother, my son," replied the old man, drawing the child towards him. "Yes, in the heaven of the blessed! It is there that all those who love Jesus go, and your mother was His faithful servant."

Franz sighed and exclaimed, "O, how good will God be if he has preserved my father, my good father! O, Grandpa, why did you let him go?"

"Franz," replied the old Christian, "your father would rather not have fought. He is so patient and kind in his heart. He is also very courageous; he has been surnamed...."

"Grandpa," interrupted the child. He was excitedly pointing with his hand towards the plain at the bottom of the steep slope. There was a narrow passage between the rocks and the woods. "Do you see those three horsemen?"

In fact, three armed soldiers were racing their horses at full gallop. They then disappeared in a thick clump of trees. The first seemed to be fleeing from the other two, who were in furious pursuit.

Erik listened, but he heard nothing. A few moments later, he distinctly saw two of the soldiers come from the woods. They hurried towards the plain, passing through the gorge through which they had come earlier.

"Alas!" said the old man, groaning, "they have killed him. They have dipped their hands in the blood of their brother."

"They have killed him? What did you say, Grandpa? Who did they kill? Is it my father?"

"No, my son. The first warrior was not Erhard. It was another man, and those are the men who have killed him. O Lord, when will you teach men to love one another? Let us go to him," added the old man.

"To the dead man?" exclaimed Franz with tremendous fear. "Grandpa, see, it is already night."

"Come, my child," said Erik, "do not be afraid. Perhaps he is alive yet. If God allows us to be of assistance to him, will you not be happy?"

"Grandpa, the woods are so dark that I don't see how we will find our way."

"Well, Franz, I will wait here. Run to the house, and return immediately with John and Matthew. Tell them that I have sent for them. Have them bring a torch and a stretcher. Be quick!" Franz was soon out of sight. In a short time he returned with the two servants. They each had a torch and carried a stretcher between them.

The child trembled while they descended over the rocks and through the woods. He feared at any moment he would step in the blood or fall over the body of the dead man. The flames of the torches wavered in the evening breeze. When the light flickered against a rock, it assumed the form of a man. As it penetrated behind the trunks of the pines, they appeared as ranks of soldiers. Franz's imagination stirred. He scarcely breathed. John walked ahead and exclaimed, "Here he is! He is dead!" Franz's heart sank.

It was a knight, one of the noblemen. Erik immediately discerned this by the shape of his helmet and the golden scarf from which hung the sheath of his sword.

Erik raised the visor of the helmet. He saw the pale and bloody face of a man who was still young. Courage and valor were etched in his features.

The knight had fallen under his horse. In the horse's side they found the point of the lance which had killed it. The whole body of his steed had covered and crushed one of his legs. The knight's right hand still grasped the handle of a sword with a broken blade.

Erik and his servants looked on for some moments. The light of the torches shone on the rich armor of the knight and on the gold-embroidered coverings of his horse. Their brilliancy seemed to open his closed eyes and revive his motionless limbs.

Franz kept close to his grandfather. He stood a little behind him. He wept softly, but not from fear. It was with grief and sorrow. He repeated, in a low voice, "They have killed him, those wicked men."

"Perhaps he is still alive," said Erik, kneeling and placing his ear to the knight's mouth. "Raise him! Loose him!" he exclaimed, rising hastily. "He is alive!''

"He is alive, he is alive!" echoed Franz. He began to push the body of the dead horse with all the force in his little frame. The three men then pushed from beneath, and they at last freed the man's leg. A stone had torn the flesh and bruised him badly. Blood was flowing freely from the wound.

"Water!" cried Erik, unlacing the knight's armor and taking off his helmet. One of the servants filled it with water at the foot of the rocks.

The kind old man made the knight as comfortable as he could. He wrapped him in the covering of the slain horse and his own coat. With one hand he supported the injured head. He used the other hand to rub lightly on his chest to stimulate the heart.

When the servant arrived with the water, Erik bathed and cooled the face and head of the knight. After a few moments, the knight sighed, and half-opened his eyes.

"Almighty God!" exclaimed Erik, "you have revived him! May it be for Your glory!"

"Amen," said his servants.

Chapter 2

An Enemy
Treated Kindly

The meek and sensitive Franz was delighted. He laughed and wept as he looked at the knight, whose cheeks had recovered some color. Franz asked him softly whether he was alive, and if he heard and saw them.

"Where am I?" the knight asked faintly, turning his eyes towards one of the torches.

"You are with God and with your brethren," replied Erik, rubbing the limp hands briskly. "Say no more now, and may God help us."

It was necessary to carry the warrior to Erik's home. The passage was long and difficult.

Erik first spread some light pine-branches on the stretcher. He then used the coverings from the horse, his own outer garments, and those of his servants. Franz begged him to take his. The old man had bound up the knight's wounded leg between strong splinters of pine. He cut the limbs with the blade of the warrior's sword, and tied it with his scarf. He then laid him carefully on the branches. The two muscular servants together raised and bore the stretcher towards the summit of the hill.

"The poor horse," said Franz, looking back. Grandfather, who carried the torch and sword of the knight, led the march homeward.

"You will return tomorrow morning," said Erik to his servants, "and take off the harness. Let the eagles and crows devour the body. Come, and may God guard and strengthen us."

The nobleman had by this time recovered his senses. He saw he was in the hands of friends. He did not doubt that the old man was a supporter of the cause he himself defended.

It was not until midnight that the convoy reached Erik's home. The journey went slowly, and more than once the master had allowed his servants to rest.

The bed of the old man himself received the wounded knight. Erik was no stranger to the art of healing wounds and fractures. He watched over his charge closely, spending the night at his side.

"Go and get some rest," he said to Franz and the servants. "May our God and Saviour keep your souls while His goodness gives you sleep."

Franz embraced his grandfather. John and Matthew bent before him respectfully. Erik remained alone, in silent vigil, near the bed. A small lamp, concealed by a thin curtain, gave all the light needed.

"You have saved me," said the knight to the old man, when all was quiet in the house. "May the Holy Virgin repay you."

"So, it is then one of our enemies," said Erik to himself, as he heard this prayer. "O, God," he said in his heart, "make your love abound in me."

"I am your friend," replied the old man affectionately. "God himself has granted me the blessing of being useful to you. I pray you, remain silent, and if possible, sleep awhile."

Erik also needed to collect his thoughts. He asked God for His spirit of peace and love. He had already supposed, upon seeing the knight's shield, that he belonged to the army of the enemy. Now he had confirmation of it. "Perhaps, perhaps," he said to himself, "I have before me the one who may have killed my son!"

The old man thus spent the moments of quiet beside the knight. He prayed to God and read His gospel of grace.

The knight slept peacefully till morning, and awoke feeling refreshed. "If it were not," he said, "for my bruised leg, I would ask for my weapons. O, how I wish to be at the head of my regiment!"

Erik sighed and gave the warrior something to drink. In a low voice he said, "Why do men hate and kill each other, while they invoke the name of Him who died to save them?"

"But," the warrior exclaimed deeply moved, "are they Christians who despise and fight the Holy Church?"

At this moment, Franz half-opened the door, and showed his pretty curly head. "Grandpa, has the wounded man been able to sleep? I have prayed to God for him," he said.

"I am much obliged to you, my child," said the knight, extending his hand to him. "Come without fear; come near. O, how you resemble my second son! How old are you, and what is your name?"

"My name is Franz," replied the child, giving his hand to the knight. "I shall soon be nine years old."

"That is also the age of my Rudolph," pursued the man. "Alas, they will think I am dead! Those villains, those cowards! Did they not see that I had no lance, and that I had a broken sword?"

"Go, my child," said Erik. "Prepare the table and the books. I will soon come to pray with you. Call all the servants."

"Will you also pray for me?" asked the knight. "If you will, pray also for my dear Hilda and our five children. O, when will I see them again?"

"Is it long since you left them?" asked Erik.

"It has been more than a week," replied the knight, with firmness. "I learned that the intrepid Erhard...."

"What...Erhard?" stammered Erik, somewhat anxiously.

"Erhard the Lion, they call him," said the warrior. "One of the chiefs of the rebels." (Erik turned pale and raised his eyes to heaven.) "I learned that this daring Erhard had joined his camp. Since it was my duty to be in the field with my soldiers, I left my family and my house. I have shown the rebels that my arm and my heart are as strong as ever."

"Did you meet this Erhard?" asked Erik, hardly daring to ask the question.

"Did I meet him?" cried the knight. "Who but myself could have need...before?"

"We are waiting for prayers," said Franz, opening the door. "Dear Grandpa, will you join us?"

The old man followed the child, and his tearful eyes soon rested on God's Book.

"Grandpa, you are crying," said Franz, drawing near to the old man. "What is the matter? You must be suffering."

"Listen to the word of consolation," said Erik, motioning to the child to sit down. "May the Spirit of Jesus Himself address it to our hearts."

He then read from the book of Psalms. He spoke gently on being resigned to the will of God. In his humble prayer he pleaded with God to remember the knight and his family. Erik asked the knight to bless him while he was in the house with them.

"Amen, amen." repeated all the servants.

Erhard left the ranks and advanced alone to meet Theobold.

Chapter 3

Love Your Enemies

"You are a God-fearing people," the knight said to Erik that afternoon, while Franz was still present with them. "Religion is a good thing."

"Anyone who loves Jesus should be happy," said the child.

"Let them love Jesus!" replied the warrior, his eyes wide. "That is what I heard last evening, when I was preparing to fight the Lion."

"Please," said Erik, "do not talk any more now. It will only increase your sufferings."

"I am not suffering," answered the warrior. "This leg is very painful, it is true. It is only a leg," he added with a smile. "Should I worry about it?"

"You fought with a lion, then, last evening?" asked Franz, curiously. "Was he very large and strong?" Franz's bright expression betrayed his innocence.

Erik would have sent Franz away, for he feared what the warrior might have to say. The latter asked that he might have permission to remain.

"Franz must become a man. My children know what a battle is. Let Franz, then, not be afraid at what I am about to say."

13

"My name is Theobold," continued the knight, "and from my earliest youth, they have called me the Iron-Hearted. I have never cried at pain, and never knew what it was to be afraid. My father, the most powerful nobleman of Bohemia, trained me. From my earliest years, I've been taught to deny cold, hunger, thirst and fatigue. I was scarcely Franz's age when I seized and strangled a furious dog. He was about to attack one of my sisters. War has been my life. This one has now lasted nearly four years, and my sword has not been idle. The Hussites and the Calixtans are mightily aware of it.''

When Franz, sitting next to the knight's bed, heard these words, he rose and walked to the other end of the room. He sat at the window and pondered the thought tugging at his heart.

"I was spending some time with my family, when I learned that the enemy was approaching. One of their mightiest chiefs had just joined them. This chief was the Lion."

Jumping to his feet, Franz said, "Grandpa, perhaps it was...."

"Quiet, my son," cautioned Erik.

"Our camps had been in sight of each other for two days," continued Theobold, "when we decided to attack. It was last evening that the battle took place.

"It lasted more than three hours. I sounded a retreat, in order to suspend the fighting, if possible. I tried to bring an end to things by staging a duel between the bravest of the enemy's chieftains and myself.

"So, our troops retired and I challenged the Lion. Without delay, he left the ranks and advanced alone to meet me." While the knight was saying this, Erik leaned against a table and rested his head on his hand.

"His sword was attached to a scarf of silver and blue. Beneath his helmet, with visor raised, curls of light hair were visible. This was a man younger than myself and of noble appearance."

"Grandpa!" exclaimed Franz, running towards Erik, "was it my...."

"Should a child interrupt an older person who is speaking?"

"Quiet, Franz," ordered his grandfather, urging the boy to sit down.

"This knight," resumed Theobold, "advanced towards me. He stopped his horse and spoke. 'Jesus has shed his blood for us,' he said in a mild but manly voice. 'Why would you shed mine? I will only defend myself,' he said, pulling down his visor and holding out his shield, 'but I will not strike.'

"I must confess that these words affected me. I was on the point of withdrawing when, fixing my eyes on the shield which he held, I saw the golden chalice."

"It was he! Yes, it was he!" cried Franz, as he ran from the room.

"The boy," said Theobold, "is still a child, and the idea of bloodshed fills him with fear."

15

"Ah!" said Erik, "Your words cause him to be anxious about his father, who is also in the army. You did not, then, spare this warrior?"

"As I have told you, the sight of the chalice provoked my fury. Crying out, 'Defend yourself,' I took my sword with both hands. With a single blow, I dashed aside his shield and split his helmet.

"My sword broke, and at the moment when the Lion fell...."

"Did Erhard then fall? Was Erhard killed?" asked Erik, deeply shaken. He hid his face in his hands, and he heard the knight say:

"So perish all who hate the Holy Church. As soon as I had struck him, his soldiers launched themselves upon ours. Five of their knights threw themselves upon me and surrounded me. I had no weapons. I had laid down my lance to combat the Lion, and my sword broke. With the fragment that remained, I was still able to strike down three men. I was alone. My people were themselves surrounded. When I realized that I would die, it was then that I fled. Now I regret it. The cowards! They did not even give me a sword. Yes, I fled towards the forest, hoping to find a branch with which I could arm and defend myself. My horse stumbled over the roots, and as a result, I fell and fainted.

"The rest you know. I owe my life to you. You have cared for me as a father would."

"So, Erhard is dead!" cried Erik, without realizing that the knight had finished his story.

"Do not feel sorry," replied Theobold. "He was an enemy of our faith. He was one of those fearsome Taborites. They deny the Holy Father and demolish sacred places."

"It was you," continued Erik, "it was you who struck him when he refused to draw his sword against you?"

"It was not I, but the Holy Virgin, who overthrew him! It was she to whom I had devoted my sword, and it broke in her service. It is thus she consecrated it. May she bless you also. You who, for the love of her, receive me as a son."

Erik said nothing in reply. He wished to pour out his tears before the Lord. He left the knight, entrusting him to his faithful and prudent John.

"Sit down," said Theobold to the servant. "Tell me who is this Prince of Peace about whom you spoke last night. Was it not you who carried me here with another servant? Was it you who was leaning towards me when we passed the threshold of this house? You were saying to me, 'may the Prince of Peace Himself receive you.' Who is this prince? Is it your master—this venerable and mild old man?"

"No, Jesus is the Prince of Peace," replied John. "For He is love, and love does not fight against any one."

"Jesus, did you say, is the Prince of Peace. Is He not with us who support His cause, and who yet fight valiantly?"

"The cause of Jesus is the gospel of His grace," said John. "Sword and lance do not support His cause. Truth and love defend it."

"Your words, John, are sermons. Where do they come from?" asked Theobold, somewhat surprised.

"He who is acquainted with God speaks the Word of God; and God is love. God will not take revenge and kill with hatred. God pardons and bestows grace," said John.

"You would say, perhaps, that God is not with me, because I take revenge on my enemies. Have they not deserved my hatred?" replied Theobold, clearly upset.

"God says this to those who know Him: 'Love your enemies. Avenge not yourselves.'" answered John.

Theobold was still astonished, saying, "Your words trouble me. Is it then a crime to destroy an adversary?"

"Cain rose up against his brother Abel. It was because the works of his brother were good. His own were evil. The Christian does not hate. The Christian does not avenge himself," replied John.

"Are you saying I am not a Christian then?" asked Theobold.

"He who is of Christ walks as Christ Himself walked," said John respectfully. "Christ went from place to place doing good. It is Christ Himself who says to His Church, 'Love one another. He who loveth is of God.'"

Theobold was silent. These words, "He who loveth is of God," had touched his heart. He was humbled and deeply affected. John was also silent. He secretly asked God to enlighten and soften the heart of the nobleman. He and Matthew had already prayed this many times.

"It is, then, not Christ-like for men to hate and war with each other?" said Theobold slowly. "Yet ungodly men deserve to burn. Are not those who imitate them the enemies of God and of the Church?"

"Can that one be a Christian," replied John, "who kindles a fire that burns a friend of Jesus? Huss and Jerome, who were delivered to the flames, loved Jesus."

"Did they not blaspheme the Holy Church?" asked Theobold.

John replied, "He who loves Jesus does not blaspheme His name. The church of Jesus has the name Jesus written on it. No, no, the true Christian does not hate others or avenge himself. Christians neither abuse their God or the Church of God."

"That is enough," said Theobold to the servant. "Leave me. I need rest and quiet." The servant went out quickly.

Meanwhile Erik had retired to his room. Like David, he wept bitterly before the Lord. With enormous sorrow, he repeated, "Erhard! my son,

Erhard! You are no more. Your father will never see you again on earth."

"Here is some one coming to us," said Erik.

Chapter 4

The Lion Returns

Franz heard the voice of his grandfather. He ran to throw himself in his arms, exclaiming, "That wicked man! He has killed my father! God has not preserved him, Grandpa. My father is dead."

"Adore God, my son," said Erik, striving to contain his grief. "Do not murmur. Especially, my son, do not become angry, and do not hate."

"Grandpa," replied Franz, with anguish. "It was he who…who killed my father!"

"No, my son. The warrior killed one whom he fancied an enemy. Theobold believed he was serving God and doing a holy work in killing a Calixtan."

"Then he must not love Jesus. The poor man!" exclaimed the godly child. "O, Grandpa, how unhappy he must be!"

"Yes, my son, he is very unhappy," replied Erik. "Do not hate him. Pray to God for him. Was it not God who brought him here? Was it not that we might speak to him of Jesus and love him? Yes, Franz, that we might love him for the sake of our Saviour."

The old man rose and advanced towards the window of his room. "What is this? What do I see in the distance, toward the rocks, at the entrance to the wood?" Franz looked also, and was sure that he saw men. "Yes, there are soldiers!" He exclaimed. "I see their helmets glistening. There are many of them, Grandpa! Are they coming to kill us also, because we love Jesus?"

"Yes," continued the old man, without looking at the child, "they are, indeed, soldiers. They are marching slowly. Ah, my child, they are our own soldiers. It is my son. It is the body of your father that they are carrying. O, God of mercy, support us at this hour!"

"I dare not see him!" cried Franz, running after the old man, who hastened to the road. "Grandpa, hide me, hide me, please!"

"Here is some one coming to us," said Erik. At the same time, Matthew and John ran out of the house. They had seen the convoy. All together they hastened to meet the soldier.

The soldier advanced, waving a scarf, exclaiming, "Praise God! Erhard is alive!"

Erik staggered, and his servants caught him in their arms. He remained weak and motionless. Franz embraced him, crying.

The soldier was all out of breath when he reached them. He took the cold hands of the old man. He said, "Rejoice, my dear lord! Bless God! Your son is alive! Here he is! Come, quickly! He wants to see you, and is calling for you."

"Grandpa, he is calling for you," repeated Franz. He pulled close to the old man, whose face was colorless. "Do not weep any more. Come, come quickly and see him!"

"O, the kindness of God! The mercy of Jesus!" said Erik, as he recovered. "Erhard is living! He is restored to me!" He leaned on the arms of his servant and walked to meet the approaching troops.

They soon heard, "My father…my son!"

"Let us praise God! I am returning to you. He has preserved my life!" Erhard had just seen his father and his child. He was making an effort to glorify the Lord with them.

He was lying on five lances tied together. Ten soldiers held five other lances crossed beneath. A shield and some cloaks supported Erhard's head. A company of soldiers followed, guarding their chief. Erik embraced his son, and blessed the name of the Lord. After Franz had also showed his tenderness, the failing strength of the chief kept him from speaking anything more. Swiftly and silently they carried Erhard into the house. He was laid in the room adjoining that in which Theobold rested.

The latter had fallen asleep after John left him. When he awoke, all was quiet around him. The soldiers, after having taken some nourishment, returned to their camp. Erhard was sleeping under the watchful eye of his joyous father. Franz repeated constantly in a low voice, "O, how good the Lord is. He has preserved my father!"

"This is a remarkable house," thought Theobold. "What kindness and goodness they show. At the same time, what seriousness and solemnity, even down to this child. How they speak of God, of Jesus, and of heaven. Am I mistaken? No, not one among them has named either the Holy Virgin or the saints."

"Can it be possible," he added, after long reflection, "that I am in the home of a Hussite? One of those Calixtans whom I hate? No, no, they would hate me also. They know now who I am. Perhaps I shall see no more of the love and concern they have shown me. There is something here that I cannot understand. I must inquire and inform myself," he said.

Erik had returned. His countenance was serene. It was with affection and warmth that he inquired if the knight felt refreshed by his sleep.

"I am as comfortable as possible," replied Theobold. "This leg pains me somewhat, and I am slightly feverish. If I could only find out how my family is! How anxious my wife and my dear children must be. The two camps will publish that the Iron-Hearted was killed."

"Reassure yourself!" said Erik. "I have taken care of that. I have notified the army that you are alive and comfortable. They do not know where you are. By tomorrow we should have news of your family. Do not worry. Be patient, and await the Lord's will. The Lord alone reigns."

In fact, at the moment of the departure of the soldiers, Erik had placed a letter in the hands of their captain to read on the way. Under oath of secrecy, he had told him all about Theobold. He charged him to inform the family and to conceal the place where he was. He also requested of the captain that a messenger bring back some reply from the family as soon as possible.

"Angel of goodness!" exclaimed Theobold with emotion he was almost too ashamed to display. "Your love confounds me. I have never seen the like up to this day. Where do you get it? Who gives it to you? Yes, all of you have the same love."

"God is love!" said Erik. "If we know Him and if He has revealed His love to us, ought we not also to love one another? Is it not in this, before everything else, that His image exists?"

"His image!" exclaimed Theobold, "the image of God! I have never heard anything like it before. I never thought that I could bear the image of God. Who has suggested to you this sublime idea?"

"Was it not for this that the Son of God purchased us by His blood? Was it not that His Spirit might renew and sanctify us, to resemble God our Father?" beamed Erik.

Leaning his forehead on one of his hands, Theobold exclaimed, "Purchased by His blood? Renewed by His Spirit? What do these things mean? These are, I am sure, the things of God and of heaven, but they are hidden from my eyes. I do not understand them. Explain them to me, please."

"Is it possible that you are unaware of the sacrifice Jesus made? Do you not know that the Saviour has shed His blood on the cross?" asked Erik.

At this question, Theobold drew from beneath his tunic of fine linen a little crucifix. It was suspended from his neck by a gold chain. After having kissed it, he showed it to Erik.

"Well, then," said the old man, "You wear upon your person a token of His sacrifice. Then why do you not rejoice in what He has done for you? Why do you not glorify Him who loved us with such love?"

"I have not yet earned it," said Theobold, bowing his head and blushing.

"Earned it!" exclaimed Erik. "How do you think that Jesus can be a Saviour, if His salvation has to be earned?"

Theobold looked at the old man for a long time in silence. At last he said, "This thought has never occurred to me before. If Jesus is a Saviour, you say His salvation is a gift. What a faith! Is that your religion?"

"I am by nature a wicked man, like all others," said Erik. "My soul rests in Jesus. My desire is to love Him, because He has loved me, even unto dying for my sins. His blood has washed my soul, therefore I know that I am saved. Can I love Him enough for such grace...."

Someone knocked at the door.

Given permission to enter, John announced that the hour for supper approached. "Our master is expected to attend the prayers."

"You will not forget me?" said Theobold, extending his hand to Erik. "Go! and may God Himself be with me as He is with you! I have much to consider."

"Theobold issued a challenge to fight me single-handedly."

Chapter 5

Erhard's Account of the Conflict

Prayers were held in Erhard's room. His wound was severe, but he would live. He needed to hear his father thank God for the enormous deliverance which had been granted him.

Their nearness to each other was carefully concealed from the two wounded men. Erik did not, therefore, pray aloud for Theobold. Neither he nor any person made the least allusion to him. It was from Erhard that his father was to learn all that concerned him. It was not until the next day that Erik called Franz and John. That afternoon they listened to Erhard' s story. Matthew remained with Theobold.

"You know, my father," said Erhard, "that I went into the battle against my will. It was a denial of faith to make war in the name of Jesus! I thought my presence would control a wrong spirit. I hoped to prevent a conflict between the two parties.

"I made my feelings known to some true friends of the Saviour. They had come to the camp with the same intentions as I. We often assembled together in my tent to arrange our plans, and especially to pray to God.

"The number for peace and forgiveness of injuries was too small, and all our efforts were fruitless. The only thing to which they would agree was that we should not be the first to attack. At the first signal of truce, we should cease fighting.

"My brethren and I had pledged ourselves before God to limit ourselves to defense. We used our arms only to protect our own lives, not to strike our enemies.

"We had learned that Theobold, one of their chiefs, had arrived in camp. He is the Lord of Rothenwald, a strong castle in the area. They call him the Iron-Hearted, because of his courage and iron will. He goes out only on retaliation and revenge. We knew also that his wife, named Hilda, was a bitter enemy of the cause of the gospel. She had treated two of our brethren very cruelly. Theobold had taken them as prisoners in a preceding fight.

"Nevertheless, my brethren and I always had a sincere desire to pray to God fervently for the welfare of Theobold and his men. Alas, he is dead, he is dead! He has gone to give an account of his soul to God. Poor, poor Theobold!"

Franz was seated beside his grandfather. He laid his hand on his grandfather's knee and looked at him knowingly. His grandfather placed his finger on Franz's lips. He kept it there, as if to enjoin upon the child the most wonderful secret. Franz, with a sigh, turned his eyes again toward his father.

"It was Theobold who started the fight. He ordered his troops forward, advancing to meet ours. We had also formed ourselves in battle array. He called us heretics and infidels, whom Heaven had cursed, and whom the Holy Virgin was about to crush beneath her feet.

"We did not reply. The conflict which then took place soon became fearsome. We were nearly equal and well-armed. It was a hand-to-hand conflict. Those of us who only defended ourselves, disabled several men. We did this by tiring them out, warding off all their blows.

"I do not know whether the Iron-Hearted saw this. About sunset, he sounded a retreat. At that instant, our army paused, thinking the battle had ended. However, it was only an interruption. Theobold issued a challenge to fight me single-handedly.

"I immediately advanced. I heard my brethren say, 'Erhard, may God preserve you. We are praying for you!'

"Theobold approached me with his visor closed. Our horses whinnied, while a cry went up from each of the two armies. Only the necessary space for the duel remained between the two sides.

"In the profound silence which surrounded us, I said aloud to Theobold, 'Jesus has shed His blood for us. He sees from heaven. He wants us to love one another. Why, Theobold, will you not hear

Him? Why will you shed my blood, and if you can, take my life?'

"'Perish the infidels!' replied the Iron-Hearted, approaching me and brandishing an enormous sword.

"'Well, then, I am ready for you,' I answered, drawing down my visor also. 'Let God be our judge. I will defend myself. I will not strike.'

"Saying these words, I held up my shield and fixed myself firmly in the stirrups of my saddle. We had both laid down our lances, and had only swords. Mine was still in its sheath.

"Theobold trembled when I spoke to him of the love of Jesus. As soon as I had raised my shield, he became furious. He seized his sword with both hands, urging his horse against mine. He struck me on the head with all his force. I fell and my helmet was split by the blow.

"See in this, my father, the hand of God, for it was thus that He saved my life. When I came to myself, I was in a cottage in the midst of the woods, surrounded by three of my brethren. They had carried me there. My wound was wrapped. I suffered only slightly, and my soul was in perfect peace. I was able to sleep a little towards the latter part of the night. Alas, it was a fatal night for the unfortunate Theobold and his men!"

"Theobold's men also?" asked Erik, almost betraying the secret of his heart.

"O, Father, the vengeance of our soldiers was terrible! As soon as I fell, they threw themselves furiously upon the enemy. Theobold, they said, was surrounded by numbers and killed in a thick wood, where he had fled. His troops were repulsed and routed, and many lives were lost. About midnight, a soldier came from one of the chieftains. He told us that they were about to seize the Fort of Rothenwald.

"Then my heart stirred. I thought of the wife and children of the unfortunate Theobold. I asked one of my captains to take a letter I had written to the family of Theobold. Disregarding my own weakness, I earnestly requested a personal favor. I asked that he safely escort the wife and family of Theobold from the castle. I told him that their lives were precious to me. Since I could not be their protector, I committed this charge to him in the name of the Lord Jesus.

"My friend immediately set out. He received from me exact instructions as to where he should escort the lady of the castle and her children. Toward day-break, I received from this brother a message. I was informed that my wishes were regarded as commands. Theobold's entire family was safe."

"Father," said Franz, warmly embracing his father, "you have done as the Saviour commanded. 'Do good to them that hate you.'"

"My son," replied Erhard, "it was my duty. I glorify God for having made it easy for me. Rothenwald is now only a smoking ruin. It was completely destroyed. My poor soldiers, how deluded they have been. How far they still are from understanding the faith of Jesus which they profess to defend."

"My dear Erhard," asked Erik, "how were you restored to me? Who brought you here?"

"It was truly the hand of God, my father. I was in the cabin of the wood-cutter, with two friends who never left me. The wood-cutter's daughter came running in, alarmed, to tell us that many soldiers were advancing towards the woods. They were in search of the house where I was hiding. 'Here they are!' she exclaimed. 'They are coming to kill you! May God save you!'

"However, these soldiers were of our own party, and came to carry me to some other place. I knew their captain. He was a God-fearing man who protected his servants. I told him that my main desire was to be with you, my father. As you see, I received my request. The wood-cutter wanted to make a stretcher for me. The soldiers said, 'Our lances and our hearts are the Lion's.' You have seen how these brave people accomplished their work of love and honor.

"My two brethren insisted upon accompanying me. I objected, saying to them, 'Go, hurry back to your own families. Many hearts are anxious for you.' As they embraced me, they committed me to the care of the faithful captain, and to our God. God Himself has preserved me, and brought me to you."

"What of Hilda and her children?" asked Erik, with keen interest.

"Thanks be to God. I have been able to send them to the house of your sister, my worthy and godly aunt who lives at Waldhaus. Her home is at a safe distance. Her heart was open to this unfortunate mother and her five orphans. You, my father, would have welcomed them yourself. A messenger from my aunt reached me while I was on my way here. I know that all is well. Alas! It is as well as it can be for a widow. She was suddenly driven from her home, despoiled of all her property. I fear she knows not yet the peace and strength which are from God."

"The thoughts of the Almighty," said Erik, rising, "are not our thoughts. His ways are not our ways. His mercies are over all His works, and His judgments are a great deep. Remain quiet, then, beneath His hand. Let His spirit teach you to wait. He can 'make the wilderness a pool of water, and the dry land springs of water,' so His holy Word declares. This Word, Jesus says, is truth."

Thereupon the old man embraced his son. "I have received you back from God the second time, dear Erhard," he said. "It is a new and wonderful joy to my heart. Happy the son," he added, with emotion, "who has been to his father only a subject of gratitude to God."

Erhard pressed the hand of his father, who then went out with Franz. On Erik's instructions, John revealed to Erhard quietly all that which concerned Theobold, to whose room the old man now hastened.

Chapter 6

A Secret Revealed

"Is there no news yet?" asked Theobold, sadly. "Night has come, and a long day has also passed. Matthew led me to hope for the speedy arrival of the messenger. He has not come. I do not know why, but I have great anxiety and anguish in my heart. Who will tell me what has become of Hilda and my children? Though, why should I fear? Rothenwald is unconquerable, and should all our enemies surround it, is it not under the protection of Our Lady? Who can take it?"

"'He who dwelleth in the secret place of the Most High,'" said Erik, "'shall abide under the shadow of the Almighty. Happy is the man who makes his refuge in the shadow of His wings, until his calamity be past.'"

"Your confidence is, then, in God alone," replied Theobold. "You do not even name the Holy Virgin."

"It is because she did not create me, nor does she keep me alive. This woman, blessed as she has been, did not purchase me with her blood and is only a creature of God. What dependence can I place upon a created being?"

Theobold said, "if God made the Queen of Heaven and the angels, and gave all power to them...."

"Sir!" interrupted Erik, "it is Jesus, the Eternal Son of the Father. It is the King, sitting on the holy mount of Zion, who said, 'all power is given to Me in heaven and on earth.' These words He applied to Himself. Beware then, for the love of your soul, of attributing this authority to Mary. Remember how, on one occasion, the Lord Jesus said to her, 'Woman! What have I to do with thee?'"

With this, Erik approached Theobold. He looked at him affectionately, as he pressed his hand. He said, "May God Himself be with you, and strengthen your heart. Tomorrow, certainly, we shall have news of your family. We know it will be good news, if it is the will of God. God, dear Theobold, is love."

With that, Erik went out. Matthew came to sit with the knight, whom he was to tend during the night. He had been instructed in what to say about the arrival of Erhard.

The night drifted away, and Theobold could not sleep. He was suffering, and sometimes groaned. The name of Hilda was continually on his lips.

Matthew did not cease to pray to God in his heart that he would visit this soul with mercy. The knight exclaimed, "how my heart aches!"

Matthew, approaching him, said, "My lord is suffering. What can I do for him?"

"Ah, Matthew," replied Theobold, "it is my heart that suffers. I fear it will break."

"If my lord," said Matthew, gently, "could weep, it would surely bring him relief."

"Weep!" exclaimed Theobold, looking at Matthew. "Weep, do you say? I do not know what it is. I have never wept. Shall the Iron-Hearted become a woman?"

"'Jesus wept,' so it is written in the Gospel," replied Matthew. "Our good Saviour is our pattern in all things."

"Do you weep, then?" asked the knight, with visible interest. "For here you seek to do all things as Jesus would."

"At least, we desire to," said Matthew humbly. "Our noble lord...."

"Is Erik a nobleman then?" asked Theobold.

"My master is the Count of Winkelthal," was the reply.

"Did you say the Count of Winkelthal, Matthew?" asked Theobold. "Erhard, the Lion, is then his son? Do you mean to say that I am in the house of Erhard's father?"

"Erhard is the only son of my master. You will be pleased to know that Erhard is alive!" Matthew said.

"Alive!" exclaimed Theobold, extending his hands to the servant. "Tell me, Matthew, are you sure of this?"

"Erhard is living. God has preserved him, and he is here. He is near you. Yes, in the room adjoining this one!" was the surprising reply.

"Now I can weep!" said Theobold, putting his hands over his face and crying aloud.

Matthew approached him with emotion. Theobold passed his arm around the neck of the servant. He leaned his head upon his chest, weeping profusely, and saying, "Have pity on me, Matthew. My soul is crushed!"

"My lord!" said the young Christian to him. "It is God Himself who has visited you and who calls you. Fear not. Let your tears flow before Him."

"Matthew, dear Matthew!" said Theobold, clasping his hands. "Pray to God for me!"

Matthew knelt beside the bed of the knight, and poured out his soul in prayer. Theobold was still weeping when the servant rose. It was only by degrees that he became composed and, at last, fell asleep.

Chapter 7

A Joyous Surprise

The night passed quietly for Erhard. It was not until morning, after Erhard had awakened, that he and John lifted their hearts together in prayer. The servant then pronounced the fate of Rothenwald, lamenting the ruin of that beautiful and splendid dwelling.

"It is the Lord," replied Erhard. "'He casteth down and raiseth up. His judgments are over all the earth.' What bitterness for the wife, the widow of the unfortunate Theobold. Imprudent man, why did he flee? Would it not have been better for him to have submitted to numbers and be taken prisoner? He would now be living, and his house would not have been burned."

"Did his pursuers say," asked John, "that he was dead?"

"They were two of our knights," Erhard said. "I heard that their intention was to capture him. They called to him repeatedly, and at last in the wood, pierced his horse with a lance. They hoped to be able to take him prisoner. However, they said that, in falling, the horse had crushed its rider. His head was struck against a rock and he was killed

43

outright, was their account. The Lord only knows whether it was so. Ah, the poor widow and her helpless orphans!"

"So, my lord would have defended him, had he been able?" John asked, deeply moved.

"I would have preserved his life at the peril of my own," Erhard said earnestly.

"You would have preserved the life of your enemy?" John repeated.

"Does John forget the words of God? Does he not yet know that 'if we love those who love us', we are just like the Publicans and men of the world?" Erhard implored.

"Erhard the Lion will therefore bless the Lord to learn that the Iron-Hearted is alive and found. He was taken from the spot where he fell."

"John! Is that the truth?" cried Erhard, seizing his servant's arm.

"It was I, my lord, who held the torch which illuminated the dark forest. It was between the trunks of the oaks and pines that I first saw a horse stretched over the motionless body of a warrior."

Erhard raised himself on his elbow. "This warrior...," he began.

"Was the warrior Theobold!" was the firm reply. "Yes, my lord, it was the very one who thought that he had struck your death-blow."

"Who directed your steps in the dark?" asked Erhard.

"God, Himself," said John. "What a work of His wonderful love! Yes, God Himself guided your noble father and your son to the Stag Cliffs. At that moment, Theobold fled from the two knights. He passed through the gorge into the woods. Your father then sent for Matthew and myself to go down there to search for him."

"My father, sent from God to the murderer of his son!" exclaimed Erhard in amazement. "How wonderful are the ways of the Most High! John, did you not say that he was dead?"

"We thought so at first," said John. "Your godly and gracious father, my lord, knelt and touched the body. He called out, 'He is alive!' and with our assistance he freed him. He stretched him out on the mossy ground and called for water. Your own father bathed and refreshed his face and all the while glorified God."

"Theobold is living!" Erhard exclaimed, lifting his tear-filled eyes toward heaven. "Who will make it known to his wife and children?"

"Your father, my lord, has seen to that. He commissioned the captain who brought you here to inform them of his safety. She is still ignorant of his whereabouts," said John.

"Where is he?" asked Erhard.

John turned, and pointed to one side of the room. He said, "Behind that wall, my lord, Theobold is in your father's bed." At this, Erhard clasped his hands, praying and praising God.

Franz, who had just entered, softly approached his father. He said to him with tenderness, "Hello,

Papa, have you slept well? It is I, Papa! It is your little Franz! Will you not hold me?"

"My son," said Erhard, placing one hand upon the shoulder of his child. "If you only knew how good the Lord is."

"Yes, dear Papa," said Franz. "God is good since He has preserved you."

"He has also preserved Theobold," added the father.

"Theobold, Papa! The knight who was dead, whom Grandpa restored by the goodness of God, do you know him?"

Franz looked at John, as if to know whether he might continue. His father, who saw the look, said to him, "Yes, dear child, I know him. I know that God has entrusted him to our care. Franz, remember that even an enemy has a claim on our love."

"Yes," continued the child. "Like the good Samaritan, we should love him and bind up his wounds. Papa, that is what Grandpa did the other night in the woods. I cannot tell you how afraid I was at first. Think, Papa, a dead man and blood! Now this knight is so good to me! I have just been to see him with Matthew. He wept as he embraced me."

"Theobold wept and embraced you, my son?" asked the father.

"Yes, dear Papa," he replied. He even said to me, placing his hand on my head, "May the God of your father bless you and make you to be like Him."

"Franz, did he say that to you?" asked Erhard, obviously touched by this remark.

"Yes, Papa," said Franz. "When I was coming away, he called me back. He gave me this flower. Then he said, 'Franz, go to your father and tell him that Theobold sent this.' He was weeping. Here it is. I did not dare to give it to you at first, because I did not know whether John...."

"Let me embrace you, my child," said Erhard. "Go, and tell my good father that I would like him to come."

"Papa," said Franz, "Grandpa would have come earlier. He went away in the night with two servants in a carriage."

"My father went away in the night, Franz? Do you know where he has gone?" Erhard asked.

"No, Papa," Franz replied. "Only he said when he set out that when I awoke, I would hear him. He went by the way of the meadowland."

"He must have gone to Waldhaus," said John, "since the meadowland is on the direct road to the castle."

All that has happened is the fruit of Christian love. Love is active, fervent, and does not put off until tomorrow the good that should be done today. Theobold's wife, whom God afflicted, needed strong consolation. Erik was hastening in the name of his God to comfort Theobold's wife who thought he was dead.

❧

"Please forgive me in the name of God alone!"

Chapter 8

Enemies United

Erhard did not at first reply to John, because something was troubling him. "John, God has given you wisdom," he said to the servant, having sent away his son. "Go, therefore, now, to this knight and convey my greeting to him in the name of the Lord. You will also say to him that my desire, my true and cordial desire, is to come to him. Say nothing of my father."

John hastened to the room where Theobold rested. He said to the servant, "John, I have not seen your master today. Is he sick?"

"My master," said John, "is not in the castle just now. My lord, you must know that God is now displaying His goodness."

"To me, John? I know that Erhard is living. He is here and I know he is near me."

"Does my lord also know that a disciple of Christ can love an enemy?" John replied.

"I was ignorant of it," Theobold said. "I have learned it here. John, you can tell me everything without fear. Do you know whether Franz took the flower to his father?"

"Yes," said John, "and I know that his father blessed God when he received it. His one main desire is that the Baron of Rothenwald...."

"Just say Theobold. And you may also say, his friend, his humble and repentant friend," Theobold interrupted.

"Franz's father says to the most noble Theobold that the cordial desire of his heart is to visit him without delay," responded John.

"Erhard! Erhard!" exclaimed the knight. "Do you hear my voice? Why can I not come to you and ask you for your pardon?"

"Theobold," a voice responded through the partition. "I am coming! John! John!"

The servant immediately went out. Theobold remained with his eyes fixed on the door, until he heard the steps of Erhard and of his servant. Then his heart failed him. He covered his face with his hands. Erhard entered and approached the bed. "Theobold, what a joy this is! It is beyond my strength. May God support us at this hour," he said sitting down. At these words John left the room, breathing a jubilant, "Amen."

"It was I, it was I who struck you!" exclaimed Theobold. His hands were bathed with the tears that covered his face. "Erhard, it was my sword that made this bleeding wound! Please forgive me in the name of God alone! Erhard, forgive! Forgive one who would have been your murderer!"

"Let our tears and our hearts mingle," said Erhard, embracing Theobold. "Bless this wonderful God who sees us and Who has brought me to you!"

"To me!" exclaimed Theobold, looking at Erhard, with color rising in his cheeks. "Ah, that bandage, that wound!" He began to weep again.

"But for this wound," replied Erhard, passionately, "would you be here, and would Theobold ever have become my friend?"

"Yes, thy friend, noble and charitable soul!" repeated Theobold. "Erhard, when I approached to kill you, you said to me, 'Why would you shed my blood and take my life?' Today, here is my blood and my life! They belong to you. I call upon God, who now hears me, as a witness."

"How wonderful are His ways!" said Erhard. "What a wonderful Providence it is Who has united us. You, the Iron-Hearted, and me, the Lion!" he said, smiling broadly. "Did the Baron of Rothenwald think, three days ago, that he would lay in the bed of the Earl of Winkelthal, peacefully smiling at the words of a Calixtan?"

Theobold reddened. This last word had surprised and disturbed him. He paused to control the secret indignation of his soul. He said, "I did not know that peace and charity could be found in these lofty towers and enormous walls. I was told, Erhard, and I believed it, that unholiness had its dwelling here."

"No, Theobold. It is the Word of the Lord and the love of Jesus that we trust. These rule and comfort our hearts."

"Yours, yes," said Theobold. "I believe it. I see it hourly. These Taborites, Erhard, and their ferocious and cruel leader, Ziska, do they know the name of Jesus? They continue to persecute the Holy Church?"

"You have seen them, Theobold, only at a distance," was Erhard's reply. "You do not realize that it was for the cause of Jesus and for His holy gospel that the days of John Huss were ended at the stake."

"Were not this Huss and his friend Jerome infidels?" Theobold asked, taken aback.

"Theobold, how could John Huss be an infidel?" replied Erhard. "When the sentence that condemned him to burn was read to him, he immediately threw himself on his knees. He prayed, 'Lord Jesus, forgive my enemies! Forgive them, for the love of Thy wonderful mercy and goodness.'"

To which Theobold replied, "Erhard, did John Huss, indeed, say that?"

"Yes, he did," was the reply. "John Huss knew Jesus Christ as Saviour. Like Jesus, he prayed for his murderers. No, Theobold, he who loves unto death and who can pray for his executioners is not an infidel."

"Hilda! Hilda!" exclaimed Theobold, groaning. "What have you done, and what have I done? Our poor prisoners! What injustice!"

"Your heart is oppressed, Theobold. Does some sorrowful remembrance distress you?"

The knight was about to reply, when a knock came at the door. Erik opened the door, holding Franz by the hand.

"Here they are!" said the old man to the child. "Look, Franz, and see whether this nobleman hates your father. See if what John told me was not true! This dear child," he added, "had some fears for his father, for he now knows all, Theobold."

"Come, Franz, and give me your hand," said Theobold gently. "Come, my child, and forgive me also. Oh, how I need forgiveness from every heart here! Will you not forgive me, Franz?"

Giving his hand to the knight, Franz said, "I love you, because my father loves you."

"Well, my son," said Erik. "Find John, and tell him to ready my horse and prepare to accompany me."

"Are you about to leave us again? Will it be for long?" asked Theobold.

"It is on your behalf, dear Sir, that I must now depart. The messenger that we were expecting did not come. I feared that my message had not reached your dear Hilda. I, therefore, went myself to tell her of your welfare."

"Is it possible? Tell me if all is well with her!" exclaimed Theobold.

"Thanks to God, Hilda and your precious children are well, very well," said Erik. "She had been anxious until last night. My message did not reach her until then. The messenger, who did not set out until daybreak, was detained on the way. I met him and bring you more than he would have known himself."

"She knows, then, that her husband is...with the Count of Winkelthal?" stammered Theobold.

"Hilda knows that her husband is with his friends, and she blesses God with us," Erik replied.

"Theobold," added Erik, "there should be no differences between us. Jesus Christ will unite us by His grace."

"He has already done so, has He not?" was the jubilant response. "The old father bound up with his own hands the wounds of a stranger—of an enemy. Then he bestowed upon him all the treasures of his kindness. This was more than fatherly care to give one whose hands, he supposed, were stained with the blood of his son. May this Jesus, who makes us love, reveal Himself in my soul.

"Would you teach me to know Him, Erhard, my dear friend?"

"Theobold," replied Erhard, "he who desires to know Jesus is no longer a stranger to His love."

"Yet, my true friends, how far I am still from that love which flows in your hearts like a river! You have forgiven even me. You can love, pity, help, and console your enemies! Erhard, it is to Hilda that your father has gone. To her who caused the eyes of two of your brethren to be put out!" was Theobold's stirring reply.

"No, Theobold, no! You could not have done that!" Erhard replied, horrified.

With a deep groan, Theobold cried out, "How bad our injustice and our cruelty have been!" With tears in his eyes, he continued, "When their eyes were pierced, they stretched out their hands on all sides. They said, 'Where are you, Lord of Rothenwald, that we may take your hand and forgive you in the name of Jesus?'"

Erik then said solemnly, "Theobold, these two blind men are with me now. They knew, last evening, the identity of the knight whom we had brought in from the forest. They have already prayed to God for you many times. They have even asked John to assure you of their sincere love, before God their Saviour."

With deep repentance, Theobold cried, "Withdraw from me and leave me! Their blood has stained me. God of heaven, how severely you have punished me!"

"Do you mean to say, Theobold," asked Erhard, "that you believe us to be more loving than God is? Don't you see that it is by His grace working in our hearts that we can forgive an injury, an offense? It is by the grace that comes from that same God that we are enabled to show mercy and love to our enemies. When you turn to God Himself, He is the One who teaches His children to be loving and merciful. Now you see Him only as an angry judge, bent on revenge. You think of Him as an enemy ready to strike you down! Don't you see your problem? Don't you see that He is a God of grace, of mercy and love?"

"Erhard," resumed Theobold, with humility, "what right has a wicked man like me to expect God to forgive him?"

"The shed blood of Christ gives us the right," replied Erik, holding his Bible in reverence. He placed it on Theobold's bed. "Every man, every sinner, who reads and believes the Word of God, has the right to receive its precious invitations and promises."

"Tell me, my friends, is it by reading and believing this Bible that you learned to love your enemies?" asked Theobold, laying his hand on the Bible.

Together, Erik and Erhard replied firmly, "Yes, Theobold."

Theobold then said, "I will read it also. As God enables me, I will believe it. For if men have called me the Iron-Hearted, I now need God to soften my heart and make me His child, His ransomed one. I want His Spirit to teach me, like you, my noble friends, to imitate Jesus. I need to learn to forgive injuries and to love those who hate me!"